Amy T and Grandma B

EILEEN TAYLOR

Illustrated by Jacqui Thomas

SCRIPTURE UNION
130 CITY ROAD LONDON EC1V 2NJ

© Eileen Taylor 1994
First published 1994

ISBN 0 86201 773 4

British Library Cataloguing-in-Publication Data.
A catalogue record for this book is available from the British
Library.

Phototypeset by Intype, London
Printed and bound in Great Britain by Cox & Wyman Ltd,
Reading.

Amy T and Grandma B

Contents

For Lauren

Amy T and the new neighbour

It was Saturday morning, and that meant that Amy T was going to see Grandma B. She put both hands around the big knob on the front door and pushed hard. Grandma B always left the bolt undone on Saturday mornings, and the door clicked open.

'Yoo-hoo!' called Amy T. 'It's me, Amy T.'

'Yoo-hoo!' came the answer, and in a moment Amy was soundly hugged. 'And how's my favouritest Amy T today?' asked Grandma B.

'I'm okey-dokey. And how's my favouritest Grandma B today?' answered Amy T.

'I'm okey-dokey, thank you,' laughed Grandma B.

'I'll be off then,' said Amy's mum. And Amy T and Grandma B stood still, as the car door opened and closed, the engine started up, and the car drove off down the street.

'What are we doing today then?' asked Amy T.

'Why don't we sit down and swap news?' said Grandma B.

'I haven't done anything exciting this week. Just lots of work at school,' said Amy T. 'Have you?'

'As a matter of fact, yes,' said Grandma B. 'I have some new neighbours in the house next door, and there's a boy about your age. When I was chatting to his mum she said Matthew might like to meet you.'

'Oh, what a pest! We got a new boy called Matthew in our class this week,' said Amy. 'I bet it's him. Well don't worry. He probably won't like me – and I won't like him.'

'Amy T!' Grandma sounded shocked. 'You don't even know the boy, and here you are saying you don't like him. That's not the girl I thought you were.'

'You don't understand,' sighed Amy T. 'Boys can be horrible.'

'And so can girls, by the sound of it,' replied Grandma B.

Just then a furry tail wafted across Amy's face, and she put out her hand to stroke Purrpuss, Grandma B's cat. He walked back and forwards across Amy T's knee, purring loudly.

'Look,' said Amy T. 'His tail is straight up except for a little bend at the top. *He* likes me.'

'I wonder if it has anything to do with the fact that you give him biscuits every Saturday,' laughed Grandma B.

Amy T gently pushed Purrpuss on to the floor.

'Come on, puss. Biscuit time.'

Amy slid off the sofa and went into the kitchen. On the windowsill was a plastic dish and beside it was a box of biscuits. Grandma B always kept them in the same place so that Amy would be able to find them. Amy carefully tipped the box and then felt how many biscuits were in the dish. Purrpuss was stretching up with his front paws on Amy's knees, meowing.

'Here you are, greedy chops,' said Amy T, as she put the dish on the floor. Straight away Purrpuss crunched and cracked the biscuits.

'Would you like a biscuit too?' asked Grandma B.

'You mean a cat biscuit?' asked Amy.

'Hmph!' snorted Grandma B. 'I think you

get cheekier every Saturday. Try opening the flowery tin. Chocolate digestives might taste better.'

Grandma B had tins of all shapes and sizes, and the one she called the flowery tin was the one that Amy called the 'tray' tin, because the lid had an edge sticking up all round, just like a tray.

'Shall I bring you one?' she called to Grandma B.

'Yes please. Bring them through on the lid.'

After Amy T and Grandma B had eaten their biscuits, Grandma B got up.

'I need some help with the kitchen bin please, Amy.'

Amy T went into the kitchen and held the lid of the swing bin while Grandma B pulled out the plastic sack. Then they both went out into the back yard.

'The dustbin is next to the back gate,' said Grandma B.

Amy T ran her hand along the high wall that separated Grandma B's back yard from the yard next door. It was a very rough wall and sometimes little bits of mortar fell out from between the bricks. Just as she reached the end Amy heard someone humming. She stopped and listened carefully. The sound was coming from the other side of the wall.

'I wonder who that is?' whispered Grandma B and tucked Amy's hand under her arm. 'We'll just step out of the gate.'

They went into the cobbled back lane.

'Hello, Matthew,' said Grandma B. 'I thought it must be you.'

'Hello,' said Matthew.

Amy couldn't think of anything to say. She really didn't like boys much. They were always hurtling around the playground or kicking balls at her head. And they seemed to shout instead of speaking. She was wondering whether she could tiptoe back into Grandma's yard when Grandma B said,

'Did I see the removal men unload a cage when you moved in?'

'Yes,' said Matthew. 'That's for my angora rabbit.'

Then Amy T did speak. 'I've never seen an angora rabbit. Could I come and look at him?'

There was a tiny pause, then Matthew said, 'But you *can't* see him. You're blind.'

'So what!' snapped Amy T. 'I see with my fingers, don't I?'

Grandma B cleared her throat.

'*I* would like to feel how soft he is,' she said, in her most persuasive voice.

'My rabbit is a "she",' said Matthew. 'I'll get her out if you really want.'

'Please', said Grandma B. And she gave Amy T's hand a sudden little shake. Amy T knew that shake. It meant 'Behave yourself – or else!'

'You can come into the yard if you want,' said Matthew. 'I'll have to shut the gate in case Snowy tries to run away.'

Amy T and Grandma B stepped up into Matthew's yard and stood quietly while he unfastened the cage door.

'Oh, she's quite beautiful,' said Grandma B. 'Look, Amy.' And Grandma B put Amy's hand very gently on the back of the rabbit that Matthew was holding.

When Amy T ran her fingers through the deliciously soft fur she forgot that she didn't like boys.

'Oh, wow!' she whispered. 'She's wonderful. What long ears she's got!'

'All the better to hear you with,' growled Matthew.

Amy chuckled.

'And look what a wiffly nose she's got.'

'All the better to smell you with,' Matthew growled. 'Why don't you feel her teeth?'

'Do you think I'm daft?' laughed Amy T, taking her hand away rather quickly. 'Why is she called Snowy?'

'Because she's all white, silly,' said Matthew.

'Don't you call me silly,' snapped Amy T.

'Oh you two,' sighed Grandma B. 'Snowy is as soft as the snow, as well as being white, isn't she?'

'I suppose so,' said Matthew. 'I hadn't thought of that.'

'You wouldn't,' muttered Amy T.

'I'd better put her back now,' said Matthew. 'She's shivering.'

Matthew clicked the padlock shut on the cage. 'You can give Snowy a piece of carrot if you want,' he said to Amy.

Amy T held out her hand and took a long, thin carrot. She wiggled the carrot until it squeezed through one of the spaces in the wire netting, and then she felt it being tugged from the other side.

'She's eating it now,' laughed Amy T. 'She's nearly as noisy as Purrpuss with his biscuits.'

'Is Purrpuss a cat?' asked Matthew.

'Clever!' said Amy T. 'He's Grandma B's, but I share him.'

'You can come and see him if you like,' said Grandma B.

Matthew hesitated.

'Were there some chocolate biscuits left, Amy?' asked Grandma B.

Matthew decided he would go.

A few minutes later Matthew and Amy T were sitting in Grandma B's house, stroking

Purrpuss. Matthew had already eaten three biscuits in a very short time.

Grandma B was sitting on her old rocking chair. The big curly springs on the bottom of the rockers squeaked as she rocked.

'Fancy us being in the same class at school, and you being Grandma B's neighbour,' said Amy T.

'You talking about neighbours reminds me of a story about a good neighbour,' said Grandma B. 'It's a story Jesus told about a man who was attacked by robbers when he was on a journey.'

'Oh, Grandma B, I know that one,' said Amy T. 'The man was very hurt and was left by the side of the road. Two men came along but they didn't help him.'

'That's right,' said Grandma B. 'At last a Samaritan came along – he lived in a place called Samaria – and when he saw the man lying injured by the side of the road, he went over to him.'

'I remember,' said Amy T. 'He had a donkey.'

'He did,' agreed Grandma B. 'After he had bandaged the man he put him on the donkey and took him to a small hotel. He looked after him and even left money with the hotel-keeper when he had to leave next day.

'Now then. Who do you think was a good neighbour to the hurt man?'

'That's easy-peasy, lemon-squeezy,' said Matthew. 'It was that last man – the one from some, some . . .'

'Samaria,' said Amy.

'You're right,' said Grandma B. 'And

Jesus wants us to care for all people because everyone is our neighbour. And that includes boys, Amy T!'

Amy suddenly began to giggle.

'What's so funny?' asked Matthew.

'I just thought that if everyone is my neighbour, I'm glad they don't *all* live next door in your house. It would be a terrible squash!'

Amy T is sad and glad

'Yoo-hoo! It's me, Amy T,' called Amy T as she pushed open the front door.

'Yoo-hoo!' came the reply. 'And how's my favouritest Amy T today?'

'I'm okey-dokey. And how's my favouritest Grandma B today?' asked Amy.

'I'm okey-dokey too, thank you,' said Grandma B.

But something was wrong. Amy T knew from the sound of Grandma's voice. It wasn't as bubbly as usual.

'What's the matter, Grandma?' she said. 'You sound sad today.'

'Well it's nothing too bad,' said Grandma

B. 'It's just that Purrpuss hasn't been in for two days, and I can't find him anywhere.'

'Oh, Grandma B. You mean he's lost. Oh, poor Purrpuss! Have you looked all through the house?' said Amy T. 'You know how he likes to hide in cupboards.'

'I've looked everywhere I can think of,' sighed Grandma B. 'I just don't know where he can have got to.'

'Shall I help you look?' asked Amy T.

'I don't think he's anywhere near,' said Grandma B. 'I've shaken the box of biscuits, and you know he always comes running when he hears that.'

Amy T squeezed Grandma B's hand. 'Don't be sad, Grandma. He might come back today.'

'He might indeed,' said Grandma B. 'But I have some washing to get on with, so why don't you take a carrot round to Snowy?'

'That's a good idea,' said Amy T. She shouted over the wall to Matthew, and then followed the rough brick wall all the way to the bottom of Grandma B's yard. She opened the gate with the latch and followed the lane wall until she came to the next gatepost.

'Hello,' said Matthew. 'I've opened the gate for you.'

'I've brought a carrot for Snowy. Can I give it to her?' she asked Matthew.

'All right then,' said Matthew, and he opened Snowy's cage. 'Where's the carrot?'

'I want to give it to her,' insisted Amy.

'You can, you can. Keep your hair on,' said Matthew.

Amy felt a gentle tug on the carrot and knew that Snowy was nibbling the end. Everything in the yard was very still and quiet except for the sound of Snowy's teeth on the carrot.

And one other very faint sound!

'Listen,' said Amy excitedly. 'Can you hear something?'

She and Matthew stood very still. 'There it is again!' shouted Amy.

'I can't hear anything,' said Matthew. 'What is it? Little green men from outer space?'

'Oh, be quiet,' said Amy. 'I can't hear if you keep talking.'

'What did you hear?' demanded Matthew.

'I heard a meow,' she said.

'Well then, it was probably a cat,' said Matthew patiently.

'You don't understand,' shouted Amy. 'Grandma B has lost Purrpuss.'

'Why didn't you say so?' said Matthew, suddenly interested. 'Where's the sound coming from?'

Amy T put her head on one side and listened intently.

'It's coming from over there,' she said, pointing out of the gate.

'That's the lane,' said Matthew.

'No,' said Amy. 'The sound is further away than that. Quick, get Grandma B!'

Matthew put Snowy back in the cage and then ran out of his yard and up to Grandma B's back door. He banged on it loudly.

'Come quick!' he said. 'Amy wants you.'

'What has she done now?' asked Grandma B, drying her hands on her apron as she hurried down the yard after him.

Amy was standing at Matthew's gate.

'I can hear a meow, Grandma B. It's coming from over there.'

Grandma listened very carefully. 'I can't hear anything,' she said. 'Are you sure?'

'Of course I am!' shouted Amy T. 'Come on!'

Amy T, Matthew and Grandma walked slowly up the lane, stopping every now and then to call, 'Purrpuss.'

'Listen,' cried Amy T. 'It's getting louder.'

'I can hear it now,' said Grandma B excitely. 'It's coming from one of the yards on the other side of the lane.'

Matthew was ahead of them. 'I think it's this yard,' he called. 'The meowing is really clear now.'

'That silly cat must be shut in a shed,' said Grandma B. 'We'd better go round to the front of the house and see if someone will open the door. Let's see now. The number on the gate is twenty-two.' And she and Amy T and Matthew all walked to the end of the lane and round to the front of the houses.

'Eighteen, twenty, twenty-two,' counted Grandma B as they walked along. 'Here we are.'

Grandma B rang the doorbell of number twenty-two. When a young lady answered the door, Grandma B explained that there might be a cat locked in the shed in her yard.

'Oh, dear,' said the young lady. 'We haven't been out to the shed for a couple of days. Come through and we'll check.'

Grandma B, Amy and Matthew all went into the house. They followed the young

lady through her kitchen and into the yard.

'I'll just unlock the door,' said the young lady. The very second the door opened, there was a scrabbling, and the noise of claws on brick, as a cat shot out of the shed and straight over the wall.

'My word!' laughed the young lady. 'He was keen to get out.'

'Thank you so much,' said Grandma. 'That was Purrpuss all right. It looks as if he's gone straight home,' and she squeezed Amy T's hand.

'Hurray!' shouted Amy T.

'The great detective solves another case,' murmured Matthew.

'I'll let you out into the back lane,' said the young lady, and soon Grandma B, Amy T and Matthew were in Grandma B's yard.

'There he is,' said Matthew. 'He's at the back door.'

'You rascal,' laughed Grandma B as she bent to pick up Purrpuss. Amy T buried her face in Purrpuss' soft fur.

'You naughty cat,' she said. 'You made us all sad.'

'But we're not now,' said Grandma B. 'First I'll feed Purrpuss, then we'll have a lemonade to celebrate.'

A little while later, Matthew and Amy sat drinking lemonade. Purrpuss jumped up on Grandma B's knee, and started washing himself.

'Amazing that you heard the meow,' said Matthew to Amy. 'I couldn't hear it until we got much nearer.'

'Not so amazing really,' said Amy T smugly.

'Amy T uses her ears more than you and I do,' said Grandma B. 'I'm so pleased that she found Purrpuss for me. In fact Purrpuss going missing reminds me of something.'

'Oh-oh,' said Amy T. 'That means a story.'

'You're right,' laughed Grandma B. 'But it isn't a story about a lost cat. It's a story about a lost sheep. D'you remember it?'

'It's my absolute favourite,' said Amy T pulling her legs up on to the sofa.

'Well,' began Grandma B, 'this is a story that Jesus told about a man who had a hundred sheep. He cared for his sheep, just like we care for Purrpuss. Each day, after they had been out eating grass, he counted them as they came back into the sheepfold. One night, as the man counted them through the gate, he didn't count to a hundred. He only counted as far as ninety-nine. There was one sheep missing.'

'I bet he didn't count properly,' said Matthew, knowingly.

'I think he probably counted again,' said Grandma B. 'And because he knew all his sheep, he even knew which one was missing. But it was night-time. What should he do?'

'If it was me I'd go home and leave that silly sheep till the morning,' said Matthew.

'Oh, you wouldn't,' said Amy T, shocked.

'Well, all right,' shrugged Matthew. 'Maybe I *would* go and look for it.'

'That's just what the shepherd did,' said Grandma B. 'He set off into the night and searched and searched for the sheep that was lost. And . . . he found it!'

'Did he *hear* it bleating?' asked Matthew.

'I don't know all the details,' laughed Grandma B, 'but I know that the shepherd was so happy that he carried the sheep home, and called all his neighbours in to celebrate with him, because he had found his lost sheep.'

'With lemonade?' asked Matthew. 'Did they celebrate with lemonade?'

'I doubt it,' chuckled Grandma B. 'It was a long time ago. Jesus said that all of us are like sheep and he is our shepherd. He doesn't want us to go away from him like that sheep went away from the shepherd.'

'I don't think I would ever want to be lost from Jesus,' said Amy T. 'But I suppose Purrpuss didn't want to be lost either.'

'No he didn't,' laughed Grandma B. 'He's too fond of a warm fire and a plate of fish!'

And Purrpuss washed behind his ears, and purred.

Amy T and the church flowers

'Yoo-hoo!' shouted Amy T one fine Saturday morning, as she pushed open the door. 'It's me, Amy T.'

'Yoo-hoo!' replied Grandma. 'I'm in the kitchen.'

Amy T walked through the living room into the kitchen.

'What are you doing in here?' asked Amy T. 'I can't smell any baking.'

'Come and see what's on the table,' said Grandma B.

Amy put her hands on the table. 'Flowers. What are they for?'

'It's my turn to do the flowers for church,'

said Grandma B. 'Do you know what kind these are?'

Amy T felt along some rather thick stems. At the end were very smooth petals that made a cup shape. She put her finger into the cup and found something sticking up.

'These aren't daffodils,' said Amy T. ''Cos daffodils have petals round the cup shape and these flowers don't.'

'These are tulips,' said Grandma B. 'There aren't any flowers in my garden yet, so I bought these at the shop. Keep your coat on, and I'll just get my bag.'

The church Grandma B went to was not far from her house and soon Amy and Grandma were in a little kitchen where cups of tea were made after church services.

'Let me see what kind of vases there are in the cupboard,' said Grandma B. 'We'll need a big one so that the tulips can stand up tall. Each flower is red and yellow, and when they open out they will look like my coal fire when it's really blazing away.'

Amy T loved Grandma B's fire. It was

cosier than sitting next to a radiator, but Amy's mum said that coal fires were a lot of work, and made more dust, so they had central heating. If the flowers were going to look like the fire, Amy T was sure people would enjoy them.

Grandma B had chosen a vase that was the shape of half a circle, with a flat piece at the bottom.

As Amy was examining the vase she suddenly drew her hand back. 'What's this wire doing in here?' she asked.

'Oh, sorry! Did you prick your fingers?' asked Grandma B. 'I should have warned you. That's wire netting, crumpled up so that the stems of the flowers can slide through the gaps, and stand upright.'

Amy T lifted one of the tulips and felt for a space in the wire netting. Then she pushed very gently until the stem would not go any further.

'Is that all right?' she asked.

'That's marvellous,' said Grandma B. 'You keep pushing in the tulips, and when

you are finished I'll fill in the spaces with
the leaves.'

Amy took great care to spread the tulips
in the vase and when the last one had
gone in she ran her hands through the
stems.

'There you are. They are quite straight.
Not one of them is droopy.'

'You've made a good job of that,' said
Grandma B. 'Now I'll put in the leaves.'

Grandma B was just putting in the last of
the leaves when the door opened.

'Hello. I wondered who was in here. I've just finished cleaning the church.' It was Mrs Edwards, the caretaker. 'Now those *are* bonny tulips. Shall I put them on the table for you before I lock up?'

'That would be kind,' said Grandma B. 'Then I can clear up all these bits of leaves and we'll be off.'

Later that day Amy T and Grandma B were wondering what to do before Amy's mum came for her.

'I liked doing the flowers, Grandma B,' said Amy T. 'Have you got any more?'

'I'm afraid not,' said Grandma. 'At this time of year I have to buy flowers from the shop. But wait a minute. I *do* have a bunch of dried flowers your mum and dad gave me for Christmas. I've never got round to arranging them. We could do those.'

Amy T was pleased to help, especially when she found that there was a special kind of hard foam to push the flower stems into. At last there were no flowers left to be pushed in, and Grandma B found a basket, just the right size for the block of foam to sit in.

'Just one more thing to do,' said Grandma B and she tied a bow of silky ribbon around the handle of the basket.

'I'll take it through to the kitchen and put water in it,' said Amy T.

Grandma B laughed. 'Oh no, don't do that. These are *dried* flowers. They don't need water.'

'Just like tulips?' asked Amy T.

'No, no,' said Grandma B. 'They must have water or they will die.'

Amy T thought for a minute. 'Why didn't we put water in the vase this morning, Grandma B?'

'Oh, no!' exclaimed Grandma B. 'Didn't we? Oh dear, now I remember. Mrs Edwards took them through, and I forgot that we hadn't put water in. Oh, Amy T, they'll be spoiled. And the flower shop is shut now.' Grandma B sounded quite cross.

'They might not have died yet,' said Amy T, hopefully.

'We'll go and see right now,' said Grandma B.

As soon as they opened the door of the church Grandma B exclaimed, 'Oh, just look at them. They're ruined!'

Amy T and Grandma B walked quickly down the aisle to the table. Amy T felt the vase and then the stems of the tulips. They were quite floppy, and the flower heads had drooped right down to touch the table. She felt for Grandma B's hand and gave it a squeeze.

'Don't worry, Grandma. Nobody will mind if there aren't flowers this week,' she said.

'But I mind,' said Grandma B, impatiently. 'I'm so cross with myself.'

Then Amy heard Grandma draw in her breath. 'Just a minute Amy T, I wonder. Let's take the vase into the kitchen.'

'What do you wonder?' asked Amy T, puzzled.

'It's something I read in a magazine about reviving tulips. Let's see if it works!'

When they had put the vase on the table, Grandma B asked Amy T to take all the tulips out of the vase very carefully. While Amy did that, Grandma B was searching in the drawers for a tea towel. Then she put the tea towel in the sink and ran cold water over it until it was soaking wet.

'I'm going to wrap the tulips up in this wet cloth and stand them in a bucket of cold water,' said Grandma B. 'Can you lay them flat on the tea towel with their heads all at one end? The article said they would look like new.'

Amy T wasn't at all sure they would. The tulips felt quite limp and dead. But she did want to cheer up Grandma so she did as she was asked.

'How long will we have to wait?' asked Amy.

'I think we'd better leave them all evening,' said Grandma B. 'I'll come down to church very early in the morning and see what they're like.'

Amy T had to go home soon after that, but as she went to bed that night she wondered how Grandma B would get on with the tulips.

Next morning Amy was ready to go to church before everyone else.

'Can you take me to Grandma's soon, please?' she asked her dad. 'There's something I've got to find out.'

The very second Amy got out of the car she heard Grandma's front door open.

'How are the flow . . .?' Amy began. But Grandma B interrupted her.

'You just wouldn't have believed it,' she laughed. 'When I went this morning and unwrapped the tulips, there they were, stiff and strong as new. I put them back in the vase . . .'

'With some water?' asked Amy.

'Oh yes!' said Grandma B ruefully. 'With some water this time. And they looked lovely! Imagine that! Just soaking them in water for a few hours made them as good as new.'

'Like a miracle,' said Amy T.

'It seemed like it,' agreed Grandma B. 'Come and walk with me to church and I'll tell you a story it reminded me of.'

'Is it about flowers?' asked Amy T, as Grandma B shut her front door.

'No,' said Grandma B. 'But it is about something else that was withered up in a church. You see, there was once a man who had a poorly hand. It had become all shrivelled and weak, and he couldn't use it for anything.'

'How awful,' said Amy T. 'I would hate that.'

'Yes. It wasn't very nice for him,' agreed Grandma B. 'One day he was in the synagogue. Do you remember that was a kind of church?'

'Uh-huh,' said Amy.

'Well, Jesus came to the synagogue that

45

day, and he asked the man if he would like this hand to be better. When the man said "Yes", Jesus told him to stretch his hand out. The man did what Jesus said, and his hand wasn't withered any more, it was just as good as his other one!'

'That really *was* a miracle,' said Amy T giving a skip and a jump. 'Because I don't think his hand would have got better by wrapping it in a tea towel and standing it in water all afternoon! Do you Grandma B?'

'Oh Amy T. You are the limit,' chuckled Grandma B.

Amy T stays the night

Amy T was carrying a suitcase as she pushed the big round knob on Grandma B's front door.

'Yoo-hoo!' she called. 'It's me, Amy T.'

'Yoo-hoo!' came the reply. 'Why are you carrying a suitcase, Amy?'

'I'm coming to stay for the night,' said Amy T.

'Are you sure?' said Grandma B.

'You didn't forget, did you?' asked Amy T.

'Let me see. There are clean sheets on the spare bed, and some extra chocolate biscuits in the cupboard,' said Grandma B.

'You were teasing!' said Amy T and she put her case on the floor and hugged Grandma B round the middle.

Amy T's mum and dad were going to visit a friend who lived quite a long way away. It was too far to drive there and back in one day, so they were going to stay with their friend overnight. Amy T didn't really want to go and Grandma B said she could stay with her.

Amy T was really pleased, and just as soon as Mum and Dad had left, she followed Grandma B up the narrow stairs to her bedroom. Grandma's room was on the right at the top of the stairs, and Amy T's was on the left.

'I think I'll unpack,' said Amy T and unzipped her case. She took out a pair of pyjamas, a sponge bag, a hair brush, a T-shirt and a pair of shorts in case the weather turned warm, and *six* fluffy toys.

'Amy T!' exclaimed Grandma B. 'Why did you bring six fluffies?'

'Well, I was only going to bring one, but every time I put one in my bag the others were so disappointed that they weren't coming that I just had to bring them all!' explained Amy T. And she carefully arranged all the fluffies along the pillow.

'Now don't you forget that the bathroom is downstairs,' warned Grandma B. 'If you get up in the middle of the night you'd better wake me up. I don't want you tumbling downstairs.'

'Grandma B! You say that every time I stay the night. Don't fuss,' said Amy T. 'Your stairs have a super shiny rod to hold on to all the way down. And I know how many stairs there are.'

And just to prove it, Amy T ran downstairs as quick as a flash.

'I wish you wouldn't do that,' laughed Grandma B.

Amy had a wonderful time for the rest of the day. In the morning she went round to Matthew's and helped him clean Snowy's cage. Grandma B asked Matthew for lunch and they had fish fingers and chips, followed by ice-cream and raspberry sauce.

After lunch Matthew had to play football in the school team, so Amy T listened to some old records while Grandma B had a nap. Then they went into town. It was

market day, and Amy T and Grandma B wandered round the stalls, and bought some apples and bananas and a new hairband for Amy. It was a soft velvet one that Grandma B said matched Amy's Sunday dress.

By the time Amy and Grandma got home again it was time for tea, and when they had eaten that and cleared away the dishes, Grandma B got out her special game of Beetle. The dice had bumpy numbers so that Amy could feel them, and the Beetle was made of wood and had holes in so that she could slot in the head, legs and feelers.

'I give in,' sighed Grandma B after Amy had won for the third time. 'It's not my night for Beetle.'

Amy T chuckled. 'Come on, have another game, Grandma B.'

'I know *your* game,' said Grandma B. 'You're trying to make me forget about the clock. It's way past your bedtime.'

'Do I have to go to bed now?' wheedled Amy.

'You have to,' said Grandma B.

'Well, do I have to have a bath?' said Amy. 'I'm very clean.'

'Go on then,' said Grandma B. 'Just a wash tonight.'

It was a very quick wash, because soon Amy T was climbing the stairs to her bed-room. She moved all her fluffies off the pillow and cuddled them to her as she snuggled down. Grandma B didn't have duvets on her beds, and when Amy pulled up the sheet and blankets, they felt much heavier than her own quilt. She ran her hand over the bed and felt the shiny satin bedspread that went right over the bed and touched the floor on both sides. It had a bumpy pattern all over it. Grandma B had once explained that it was made by rows of tiny stitches, and if Amy was very careful she could feel them.

'You didn't forget to say your prayers, did you?' said Grandma B when she came up to kiss Amy.

'Oops,' said Amy T. 'Can I say them in bed?'

'All right,' said Grandma B and she gave Amy a hug and a kiss. 'And good night all the fluffies. Do I have to kiss them as well?' asked Grandma B solemnly.

'No, I'll let you off,' giggled Amy T.

Amy T listened to the squeaks on the stairs as Grandma B went back down. She said her prayers and lay in the still, quiet room, thinking about all the things she had done that day, and wondering if Mum and Dad were having a good time. Then she fell fast asleep.

Crash, Boom!

Amy T was suddenly awake. What was that dreadful noise? The house was very quiet now, but Amy hugged as many of her fluffies as she could, and cuddled down under the blankets.

Rumble – *craaash*! There it was again. Amy T hardly had the words, 'Grandma B!' out of her mouth, before Grandma B was there beside her.

'What was that?' quivered Amy T feeling a little better now that Grandma B's arm was safely round her.

'It's just thunder,' said Grandma B. 'It woke you up.'

Grandma B didn't say anything else as there was another huge peal of thunder.

'My word,' said Grandma B. 'That one was right overhead. I'm not sure *I* liked it,' and she pulled Amy T nearer.

'I've just remembered I forgot,' said Grandma B.

Amy T laughed. 'What do you mean?'

'I forgot to tell you a bedtime story,' said Grandma B.

'You could tell me one now,' said Amy T.

'As it happens,' said Grandma B, 'I know just the one. It's all about a storm.'

'Oh no!' said Amy T shivering as another peal of thunder crashed and rumbled nearby.

'Oh yes,' said Grandma B. 'The storm in my story happened when Jesus and his friends were in a boat on the sea. It was night-time, just like it is now, and Jesus was actually asleep in the bottom of the boat. When the storm began his friends were very frightened, because they thought the boat might capsize.'

'What's that?' asked Amy T.

'It means that a boat turns over in the water instead of staying on top,' explained Grandma B.

'Yeugh,' said Amy T. 'Carry on, please.'

'There was such a strong wind that the waves were very high, and splashing into the boat, and pushing it all over the place. And still Jesus slept on.'

'He must have been very tired,' said Amy T. 'This storm woke me up. What happened next?'

'Well,' said Grandma B. 'The friends of

Jesus were so scared that they woke Jesus up. Jesus asked them why they were so afraid, and then he stood up and spoke firmly to the winds and the waves. He said, "Peace, be still".' Grandma B stopped talking, and thought for a little while.

'What happened?' asked Amy impatiently.

'It was quite wonderful,' said Grandma B. 'Suddenly, the wind died down and the sea was calm. The friends of Jesus were really surprised that even the wind did what Jesus said.'

'His friends shouldn't have been scared if Jesus was with them,' said Amy T.

'Exactly so,' laughed Grandma B, giving Amy an extra big hug. 'And if you listen you'll notice something.'

Amy sat still in bed, listening and waiting. When the next rumble of thunder came, it was very quiet, almost like a loud purr from Purrpuss.

'Why has the thunder gone so quiet?' she asked, rather sleepily.

'Because the storm has passed over,' said Grandma B. 'All storms last for a while and then they go away. And now it's time for you and all your fluffies to snuggle down. Good night and God bless.'

'Good night,' murmured Amy T, as she drifted off to sleep.

Amy T has an unusual afternoon

It was after lunch before Amy T set off for Grandma B's on the next Saturday. Amy's dad stopped the car much sooner than usual.

'We'll have to leave it here,' he said. 'I can't park any nearer.'

'Why not?' asked Amy T. 'I don't want to walk.'

'You never know what you might miss,' said Dad, persuasively. 'It's a secret!'

'Oh all right,' grumbled Amy. 'I'm coming.'

Five minutes later, as they turned into the street where Grandma B lived, Amy could hear lots of people on the pavement.

'Hi Amy!' shouted Ben, who lived three doors up.

'It won't be long,' said Mrs Edwards, who didn't live in the street at all.

'I thought you were never coming,' complained Matthew.

'It's carnival day!' shouted Amy T. 'Why didn't you tell me? Oh, super, splendid!'

'Here's a chair for you,' said Grandma B, who was sitting in a garden chair on the pavement outside her front door.

Amy T sat down on a chair that really belonged at Grandma B's table.

'I remember this from last year,' she said. 'Have we got some bags of pennies?'

'Would I forget?' said Dad as he dropped two bumpy bags into Amy T's lap. 'Give one of them to Matthew.'

Amy T tipped some of her bag out and began to count how many pennies there were. But there was not time.

'Listen,' said Grandma B. 'They're coming!'

Amy T put her head on one side and listened. She could hear the thump, thump, thump of a big drum, and muffled sounds of trumpets. The noise got louder and louder until everyone shouted, 'Here they are!' and the brass band came round the corner into the street. What a glorious noise they made! Amy liked the trumpets, and the saxophones, and the drums, but she really loved the tinkly xylophone. Mum had told her last year that one of the bandsmen held it in front of him and played while he marched. Amy thought she would love to do that.

Then, above the music of the band, came the loud revving of the lorry engines as they crawled up the street behind the band.

'Look at that,' shouted Matthew. 'Oh, wow!'

'What is it?' asked Amy T.

'It's just like a circus on the lorry,' said Matthew. 'It's amazing!'

Amy T was going to ask some more, but a jingly sound was coming very close. In fact it jingled right under her nose.

Amy giggled and put her hand up to feel the money can. She dropped five pennies in.

'Thank you, kind lady,' said the person holding the can. 'Next please.'

Matthew dropped some of his pennies on the ground before they went into the tin, and he had to crawl amongst everyone's feet to find them. But it didn't matter. Everything was fun, and noise, and laughter.

While Amy could still hear the brass band going away up the street, a jazz band turned the corner at the bottom. And so it went on. As one band passed, another was on the way, and in between the bands there was the heavy drone of the lorries.

The people on the lorries shouted to those watching on the pavements, and they shouted back. And the cans jingled. So many cans that Amy lost count, and her bag of pennies was much lighter. Some of the people with the cans let her feel their strange clothes. One had a shiny wig on, and one was dressed in cardboard boxes!

'This is wonderful!' she shouted to Grandma B, as she bit into a toffee apple.

Grandma B squeezed her hand. 'There's

a troupe of tap dancers coming now.'

The parade stopped while a group of girls did a tap dance right in front of Grandma B's house.

'How do their feet make such a clicky noise on the street?' asked Amy T.

'They have small pieces of metal fixed to the bottom of their shoes, and when they kick their feet against the ground it makes that tapping noise,' explained Grandma B.

'That sounds like fun,' said Amy T, kicking her feet against the pavement.

'Hey!' shouted Mum. 'You have to have special shoes. You'll put holes in those shoes doing that!'

Amy T chuckled, and tried to keep her feet still. But it was so hard. The music kept making her feet jig up and down.

The parade seemed to go on for ever. Dad said it was just over an hour, and he was glad that he had a seat. Mum said perhaps she should go and put the kettle on. But Amy T and Grandma B and Matthew sat there until the very last lorry had gone by, and the very last jingly can was being shaken under their noses.

'Put all your pennies in now,' said Grandma B. 'This is the last can.'

'I want to keep some of them for myself,' said Amy T, putting the bag in her pocket. 'I've given a lot away.'

'Amy T!' exclaimed Grandma B. 'Put those pennies in the tin right now!'

'All right, Grandma B,' sighed Amy T, and she emptied the bag into her hand, and fed the last few pennies through the slit in the top of the can.

'I was going to buy myself a chocolate bar,' she said.

'Don't you know where all that money goes to?' asked Grandma B.

'I expect the people keep it,' said Amy T.

'No, they don't,' explained Grandma B. 'Every year all the money collected at the carnival goes to help people with no homes, or people who are ill.'

'I suppose I don't mind them having all the money then,' said Amy T, but she didn't sound too sure.

'Shall I take my chair in now?'

'Yes,' said Grandma B. 'And as your mum seems to be getting tea ready for us, I'll tell you a story you've just reminded me of.'

Amy T settled down next to Grandma on the sofa and her dad sat on the other side of her.

'It's a long time since you told me a story, Grandma B,' he said.

'As I remember, you weren't very good at sitting still,' said Grandma B.

66

'I'll make sure he sits still,' said Amy T, taking hold of her dad's hand and holding *very* tight. 'We're ready for the story now. Is it about a carnival?'

'No,' said Grandma B. 'It's about giving money away, just like you were doing in the jingly cans, and it happened a long time ago when Jesus was in Jerusalem.'

'Did they have jingly cans then?' asked Amy T, rather surprised.

'No,' laughed Grandma B. 'but when people went to the temple, there was a special place to put money in. One day Jesus was standing nearby, and he saw some rich people throwing in lots of money.'

'That was good,' said Amy T.

'Yes,' said Grandma B. 'It did look very good. But just then a lady came along. She wasn't very rich, and she only slipped in two very small copper coins.'

'That wouldn't help many people,' sighed Amy T.

'Guess what Jesus said,' said Grandma B. 'He said that the poor lady had put in more than all the others.'

'But she hadn't,' said Amy T.

'Jesus knew that the other people had a lot of money left,' said Grandma B, 'but the poor lady put in everything that she had. That was all the money she had to live on, and buy her food. He knew that she really must love God to give up even the little bit of money she had.'

Amy T was quiet at the end of the story.

'What are you thinking about, Small Fry?' asked Dad.

'I suppose the collection plate at church is a bit like that place in the temple,' said Amy T.

'I suppose it is,' said Dad.

'I see,' said Amy T. 'Well, please could I have my pocket money before we go to church tomorrow? There's something I want to do.'

'What's that, Small Fry?' asked Dad, giving her a hug.

But Amy T would not tell. She could have secrets too!

Amy T and the chest of drawers

'Yoo-hoo! Are you ready?' called Amy T, pushing open Grandma B's front door.

'Yoo-hoo! I'm coming,' said Grandma B.

'You can sit in the front,' said Amy T, as her dad opened the car doors.

'Where are you going?' asked Matthew, who had just come along the street on his bike.

'We're going to look for a new chest of drawers for Grandma B,' said Amy T.

'I wish I could come,' said Matthew.

'Why not?' said Amy's dad. 'If that's all right with your mum.'

Matthew rushed to put his bike away and

ask his mum. In no time at all he was bouncing into the back seat next to Amy.

'Are you going to the big showroom?' he asked Grandma B.

'Yes,' she said.

'Ace!' said Matthew, and he nudged Amy T. 'There's a ball pool in the showroom.'

'What's a ball pool?' asked Amy T.

'Well, it's a sort of – you know – big thing – with balls in, and you climb in and fall around.'

'What will they think of next?' said Grandma B.

Amy's dad parked the car in a space quite near the door of the showroom and they all went in.

'Let's see,' said Dad. 'Carpets downstairs, furniture upstairs.'

There seemed to be an awful lot of stairs, but at least they were carpeted and not very steep.

'Look at all this stuff,' said Dad. 'We'll be here all day.'

Amy T and Matthew followed Grandma B and Dad as they looked at lots of chests of drawers. The furniture was laid out in rooms – bedrooms, lounges, dining rooms and kitchens. Amy T was quite surprised to find that there could be so many different kinds of drawers, but after a while she and Matthew were bored.

'How long are you going to be?' asked Amy T, tugging at her dad's jacket.

'Grandma wants just the right one,' he said. 'It could be ages. Why don't you and Matthew go and find the play area? But don't leave the shop. I'll come and get you when we're ready.'

Amy T hung on to Matthew's jumper as he rushed across the huge showroom.

'Here it is,' he said. 'Look at this.'

Amy T walked round a very large box. It was made of thick foam covered in plastic. The box was open at the top and inside were hundreds of light, hollow balls.

'Come on! Climb in!' said Matthew, who was already diving amongst the balls.

Amy T heaved herself over the edge and slowly rolled in. But it didn't hurt. In fact, whichever way she fell, the balls just fell gently around her. After a while she tried jumping and tumbling. No matter what she did, she didn't hurt herself. It was strange and exciting at the same time.

'It's like being on a bouncy castle, only it's not!' she shouted to Matthew, who was sitting on the side, trying to fall in keeping his hands behind his back.

'Ouch!' exclaimed Amy T as Matthew landed on top of her. 'Watch where you're going!'

'Sorry,' said Matthew, struggling to stand up. 'This pool isn't all that big. I've been in a much bigger one.'

'Everybody out!' said Dad. 'Grandma has made her mind up.'

'Already?' moaned Amy T. 'This is ace. Why is it always time to go when we're having fun? Can't we stay?'

'If you want a lift home you'd better come now!' warned Dad.

Matthew and Amy climbed out of the ball pool and walked back to Grandma B.

'This is the one,' said Grandma B. 'Do you like it? I'm going to put it in the cupboard under the stairs.'

Amy thought it would do. It was quite plain wood apart from the drawer handles which were metal.

'Right then,' said Dad. 'We'll just go and buy this one and get it on the car.'

Amy was amazed. 'It's far too big,' she said.

Dad chuckled. 'You wait and see, Small Fry,' he said.

They went downstairs and stood near a cash register. Dad and the lady had a chat, and Grandma B took out her purse. Then they had to wait for something.

'What are we waiting for?' asked Amy T impatiently.

'For the drawers, silly,' said Matthew.

'But they're upstairs,' said Amy. 'And don't you call me silly, stupid.'

'You don't get *those* ones,' said Matthew. 'You get another set just like it from the storeroom. Here it comes.'

Amy went forwards to see the chest of drawers, but all she felt was a large cardboard box.

'*Now* you can see how it will go on the car,' said Dad. 'All the wood and screws are in the box. I'll have to screw everything together when we get home.'

'Let's go then,' said Amy. 'Bags me open the box!'

After lunch at Grandma's, Amy T's dad put the long cardboard box on the floor of the lounge. Amy and Matthew pulled off the

sticky tape that ran right along the box and opened it out.

There were several pieces of wood, some long and some short. There was a polythene bag full of screws and a sheet of instructions.

'Would you and Matthew sort out all these screws on a tray, please?' asked Amy's dad.

Amy was really good at sorting, and there were some most unusual screws in the bag. Some of them weren't like screws at all.

'That's a good job done!' said Dad, when they had finished. 'I'll check them off against the list and get started.'

Amy and Matthew sat on the floor while Dad began to put the drawers together. They handed him the different screws when he asked for them. Matthew hammered in some dowels, and Amy screwed in two large cam screws which held the back of the chest to the sides.

At last there were no more screws on the tray.

'There now,' said Dad to Grandma B. 'One chest of drawers, nearly ready for use. You just have to wait a day for the glue to dry.'

'Thank you,' said Grandma B. 'I don't think I could have made that by myself. But I *have* made some gingerbread for you all.'

Warm gingerbread was Dad's favourite and Matthew said it was scrummy.

'It always takes longer than you think to build these things,' said Dad, wiping crumbs off his trousers and looking hopefully at the

plate of gingerbread.

'It looked complicated to me,' said Grandma B as she handed him another piece. 'Just imagine if you had to make a whole world!'

'You would never have to do that,' said Amy T. 'It's already there.'

'The world wasn't always here,' said Grandma B. 'In the very beginning, God made it.'

'Wow!' said Matthew. 'Think of all the things he would need to make it. I mean, he would need rock and water and seeds . . .'

'And fur and skin and bones,' added Amy.

'That's just it,' said Grandma B. 'God didn't use anything to make the world. He created it out of nothing.'

'You're joking,' said Matthew. 'That's impossible.'

'It is to us,' agreed Grandma B. 'But nothing is impossible with God, because he *is* God. And while you're working that out, why don't you have another piece of my gingerbread?'

And Matthew didn't find *that* impossible at all!

Amy T has a day out

One Saturday Amy T didn't even get out of the car to knock on Grandma B's door. Instead, Matthew and Grandma B climbed in.

'You're both in a hurry,' said Dad, as he started the engine again.

'We didn't want to miss the train,' said Grandma B, struggling to fasten her seat belt. 'Oh, these things. They're never where you want them!'

'Let me do it,' said Dad, clicking the belt into place. 'And stop worrying. The train doesn't leave for another twenty minutes. I do wish you would let me drive you all the way.'

'Definitely not,' said Grandma B. 'It's just not a proper trip to the seaside if you don't go on the train. Isn't that right?' And she turned round to the children in the back seat.

'You bet,' said Amy T. 'I hardly ever go on a train.'

There was a crunching and rustling noise.

'Matthew, what are you eating?' asked Amy T.

'Mmmm,' mumbled Matthew. 'If I eat my picnic now, there's less to carry.'

'I told your mum that we'd go into a cafe, so I expect she's just given you emergency rations,' laughed Grandma B.

'What are those?' asked Matthew.

'What you've just eaten,' chuckled Grandma B, as the car stopped in the station car park.

Amy T and Matthew followed Grandma B into the station and waited while she bought her ticket. Then they each stepped

up to the window and said, 'One half return to Nethersands, please.'

'I'll keep my own ticket,' said Matthew when Grandma B put Amy's in her purse.

'Well, be careful with it,' warned Grandma B.

It seemed a long wait for the train. The station wasn't very busy so Amy T and Matthew sat on a seat, counting up to a hundred over and over again. Then they played 'I hear with my little ear', until the train pulled in.

The doors slid open and the children and Grandma B climbed into the train. Grandma B found seats together, with one at the window for Matthew.

'When I was your age we went on *steam* trains,' said Grandma B as the train moved off.

'I've been on a "Steam Special",' said Matthew, 'when I was on holiday last year.'

'What was it like?' asked Amy T.

'It was ace,' said Matthew. 'We went to speak to the driver, and he told me all about the engine. There was this old-fashioned kind of buffet car and we sat in there all the way back and had crisps and coke.'

'Did you get smuts in your eyes?' asked Grandma B.

'What are those?' asked Matthew.

'They're bits of soot that are puffed out with the smoke. If you leant out of the window, you could get a piece in your eye. And the trains got very dirty inside with the soot. My mother was always telling me not to touch the window ledges.'

It was funny to think of Grandma B ever being a little girl, but Amy T and Matthew hardly noticed the journey passing at all as Grandma B told them all about her holidays years and years ago.

'I can see the sea,' said Matthew. 'It's right beside the railway.'

'Nethersands, all change,' came the voice over the loudspeaker.

'Here already!' said Grandma B. 'Pick up your bag Matthew, and hang on to me, Amy T.'

There was a gate at one end of the platform at Nethersands, and it opened straight on to the beach.

'Find us a nice spot, please Matthew,' said Grandma B. 'Somewhere out of the breeze.'

Matthew found a place behind a break-water, and Grandma B took a rug from her bag and spread it out.

'Let's paddle straight away,' cried Amy T.

'Shoes off then,' said Grandma B, and she kicked off her own sandals and led the way down the beach.

'It's freezing!' yelled Matthew.

'Brrrrrrrr!' said Amy T.

Grandma B didn't say anything, but her eyebrows went right up.

'I think that will do for me today,' she said. 'Let's walk along on the edge and catch the waves as they come in.'

Amy T liked the sand. There were no little stones and it was soft and soggy under her feet. Further away from the water's edge the sand was dry.

'Let's build a sandcastle,' said Amy T.

'I'll be in charge,' said Matthew.

It took a long time to build Matthew's castle. He wanted a huge square of walls,

each wall thick enough to have sand pies all along. Amy T was very good at filling a bucket and turning it upside down to make the sand pies.

Around the edge of the castle Amy and Matthew dug out a moat, and Matthew ran to the sea with the bucket to bring water for the moat. But as fast as he poured it in, the water sank into the sand and disappeared.

'This is no good,' he said after three trips to the sea.

'What about a channel from the sea to the moat?' said Grandma B. 'The tide is coming in and the water will run up and round the castle.'

'It might work,' said Matthew, and began digging with his hands.

'What can I do now?' asked Amy T.

'You could put a shell on the top of each sand pie. But be careful! They might collapse.'

Grandma B collected some shells, and soon Amy T had quite a selection to choose from.

'The water's coming!' yelled Matthew from the water's edge.

Amy put her hand into the moat and sure enough, she could feel water swirling around.

'It's staying,' she called. 'This is the best castle ever!'

'Now what?' asked Matthew. 'The castle is perfect.'

Grandma B looked at her watch. 'How about the cafe?' she said, folding up the rug.

'Ace!' said Matthew. 'I'm starving.'

Matthew didn't talk much for the next half hour. He and Amy had a cheeseburger and a packet of fries, followed by a milk shake each. Grandma B had a cup of tea and a bun.

'Feel better now?' asked Grandma B.

'Just a bit,' sighed Matthew. 'What now?'

'Let's go back to the beach,' said Amy T.

They wandered slowly back to the beach.

'Where's the castle?' cried Matthew.

'I think that big heap of soggy sand is where it *was*,' said Grandma B.

'What's happened?' asked Amy T.

'The tide has come in,' said Matthew.

'No probs. I could build a better one if I wanted.'

'That's not an ice-cream van along there, is it?' said Grandma B shading her eyes as she looked along the promenade.

'Too right it is,' said Matthew, in his best Australian accent.

'If that means "yes", would you both like an ice-cream?' asked Grandma B.

'Too right,' said Matthew and Amy at exactly the same time.

It was difficult to choose just which ice-cream to have, and soon there was a small queue behind Amy T, who just could not make up her mind.

'I'm counting to five,' said Grandma B. 'One, two, three . . .'

'I've decided! I've decided,' said Amy T. 'I'll have a raspberry ripple.'

There were some wooden benches on the promenade and Grandma B, Matthew and Amy T sat on one to eat their cones.

'You know,' murmured Grandma B, licking ice-cream off her fingers. 'Your sand-

castle reminds me of a story Jesus told.'

'I bet I know which one,' said Amy T. 'Grandma B, let me tell it.'

'All right,' said Grandma B.

'There were two men who wanted to build a house. One built his on sandy ground because it was quicker. The other man built his house on the rock. That was much harder to do. Then a storm came and the house that was built on the sand just fell down. Kerzonk!'

'Goodbye house,' said Matthew.

'That's right,' said Grandma B. 'Jesus said that people who listen when he tells us how to live but then do what they like, are like the man who built his house on the sand. Or like your castle that looked so perfect.'

'You mean they'll go kerzonk?' said Matthew.

'Oh, you are a ticket, Matthew,' said Grandma B. 'And that reminds me. I hope you haven't lost your ticket. It's time for the train.'